W9-AGZ-146

THE ADVENTURES OF
KING
ARTHUR

THE ADVENTURES OF
KING ARTHUR

Retold by Russell Punter

Illustrated by Andrea da Rold

Series editors: Lesley Sims & Jane Chisholm

Consultant: Mike Collins

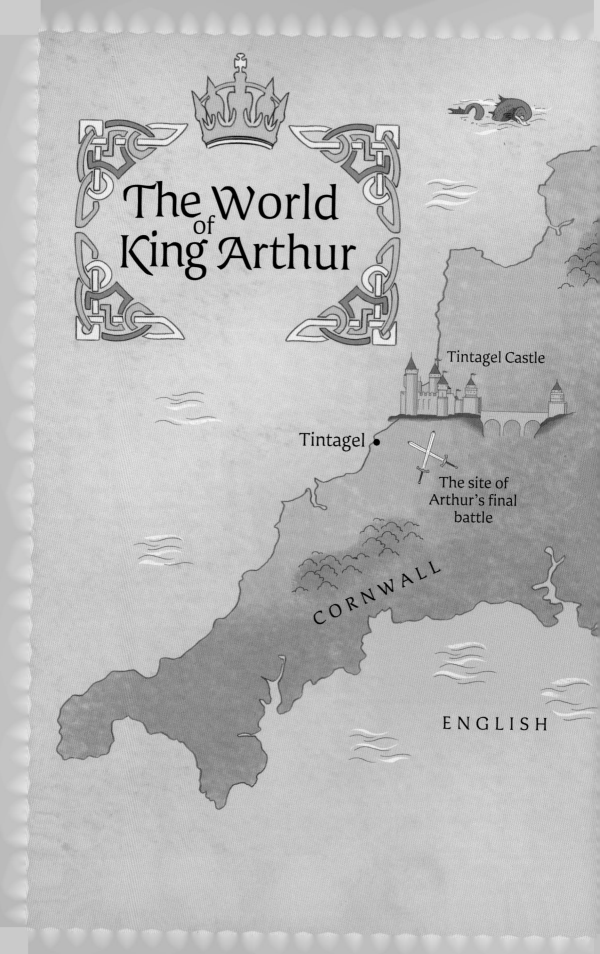

The World of King Arthur

Tintagel Castle

Tintagel •

The site of Arthur's final battle

CORNWALL

ENGLISH

SOMERSET

Arthur's resting place

DEVON

Avalon

Lake of Avalon

Camelot

Lake of the enchanted ship

Camelot Castle

Sir Damas' Castle

DORSET

Joyous Garde (Sir Lancelot's Castle)

Merlin's resting place

BRITAIN

King Pelles' Castle

London

CHANNEL

Sir Lancelot's French Castle

FRANCE

Many years ago, Britain was a thrilling land of brave knights and magnificent castles, ruled by the bold King Uther Pendragon.

While he lived, the kingdom was a safe and peaceful place. But one wise man had seen a dark and terrible future. Even now, that man was on his way to Tintagel Castle to warn the king…

9

BUT **WHY** MUST YOU TELL ME THIS?

FOR THE SAKE OF THE **KINGDOM,** SIRE.

WHEN YOU ARE **DEAD,** OTHERS WILL TRY TO **STEAL** THE THRONE FROM YOUR SON. BUT HE WILL BE **TOO YOUNG** TO FIGHT.

IF WHAT YOU SAY IS TRUE, **WHAT CAN I DO?**

LET THE CHILD BE BORN IN **SECRET.**

I'LL TAKE HIM TO A PLACE OF **SAFETY** UNTIL HE'S OLD ENOUGH TO CLAIM THE THRONE.

THE DESPERATE KING STRUGGLES WITH MERLIN'S SUGGESTION, UNTIL AT LAST...

VERY WELL...

...FOR THE SAKE OF **THE KINGDOM.**

THE WISE WIZARD'S PREDICTION COMES TRUE – THE KING SOON FALLS ILL AND DIES, AND A VIOLENT SERIES OF BRUTAL BATTLES BEGINS FOR THE CROWN...

THE KINGDOM IS THROWN INTO CHAOS...

MUCH BLOOD IS SPILLED...

BUT NO ONE EMERGES TO UNITE THE LAND.

SIXTEEN YEARS LATER, MERLIN VISITS THE ARCHBISHOP IN LONDON...

THESE ARE **DARK DAYS,** MERLIN.

NOT FOR MUCH LONGER, MY FRIEND...

I WANT YOU TO GATHER THE LAND'S **MOST NOBLE KNIGHTS** HERE, ON CHRISTMAS DAY.

KNIGHT AFTER KNIGHT TRIES TO REMOVE THE SWORD, WITHOUT SUCCESS...

IT'S A **TRICK!**

IT MUST BE **STUCK!**

NO MAN COULD SHIFT IT!

AND SO, THE BISHOP ISSUES AN INVITATION TO EVERY KNIGHT IN THE KINGDOM...

GRAND TOURNAMENT

London New Year's Day

To conclude with a contest to remove the famous sword from the stone.

A FEW DAYS LATER, AT THE HOUSE OF SIR ECTOR AND HIS SONS, SIR KAY AND ARTHUR...

WHAT ARE YOU **DOING**, KAY?

PREPARING FOR A **TOURNAMENT** IN LONDON.

YOU CAN BE HIS **SQUIRE**, ARTHUR.

EARLY ON NEW YEAR'S DAY, ECTOR AND HIS SONS ARRIVE IN LONDON FOR THE TOURNAMENT. AFTER TAKING LODGINGS AT A NEARBY INN...

KAY! THE TOURNAMENT IS ABOUT TO **BEGIN.**

I **DON'T BELIEVE IT!** I MUST HAVE LEFT MY **SWORD** AT THE INN.

I'LL RUN BACK AND GET IT FOR YOU.

BUT WHEN ARTHUR REACHES THE INN...

THE PLACE IS **LOCKED!**

EVERYONE MUST BE AT THE TOURNAMENT.

ARTHUR IS RACING BACK, WHEN...

A SWORD!

ARTHUR SETS UP COURT AT THE CASTLE OF CAMELOT. OVER THE YEARS, HE RULES FAIRLY AND WISELY, VOWING TO HELP THOSE IN NEED.

ONE DAY, A YOUNG MAN RUSHES INTO THE CASTLE COURTYARD...

WHO KILLED HIM, BOY?

I BEG YOUR MAJESTY'S HELP. MY MASTER, SIR MILES, WAS SLAIN IN THE FOREST!

A BRUTE NAMED SIR PELLINORE. HE LIVES IN THE FOREST AND HAS SWORN TO KILL ANY KNIGHT WHO PASSES.

HE HAS NO SUCH RIGHT! I WILL DEAL WITH THE ROGUE MYSELF.

ON HIS WAY TO THE FOREST, ARTHUR COMES UPON A ROBBERY...

AWAY WITH YOU, VILLAINS! LEAVE THE OLD MAN BE!

AS THE ROBBERS FLEE, ARTHUR RECOGNIZES THEIR INTENDED VICTIM...

I URGE YOU TO **TURN BACK**, SIRE. PELLINORE IS A **MIGHTY** WARRIOR.

MERLIN! LUCKY FOR YOU THAT I WAS HERE.

I'M ON MY WAY TO DEAL WITH A **KNAVE** NAMED **SIR PELLINORE.**

SO AM I. **FEAR NOT!**

BEWARE OF SIR PELLINORE'S **STRENGTH,** ARTHUR...

...AND YOUR OWN **PRIDE.**

AS ARTHUR REACHES THE HEART OF THE FOREST...

HA! DEFEND YOURSELF, STRANGER!

SIR PELLINORE, I PRESUME? I'VE COME TO TEACH YOU A **LESSON.**

BOTH MEN CHARGE AT FULL TILT...

OOOF!

CRASH!

WAAH!

THROWN FROM THEIR HORSES, THE TWO WARRIORS DRAW THEIR SWORDS...

I'LL FIGHT TO THE **DEATH!**

THE DEATH SHALL BE **YOURS!**

I KNOW WHERE A **FINER** SWORD IS TO BE FOUND. **COME!**

THE WIZARD LEADS ARTHUR ACROSS THE LAND, TO A LAKE HIDDEN ON THE EDGE OF A FOREST...

BEHOLD... **THE LAKE OF AVALON!**

HOW WILL I FIND A SWORD **HERE?**

WATCH!

ARTHUR AND MERLIN RETURN TO CAMELOT...

YOU WERE **RIGHT,** MERLIN. THIS IS THE **FINEST** SWORD I'VE **EVER** SEEN!

TRUE, SIRE. BUT THE **SCABBARD** IS **MORE** POWERFUL.

WHILE YOU WEAR IT, YOU'LL **NEVER** SHED A DROP OF BLOOD IN BATTLE.

NOT LONG AFTER, IT'S MERLIN'S TURN TO FALL IN LOVE...

BUT LADY NIMUE IS NOT AS HONEST AS GUINEVERE...

I'LL **PRETEND** TO LOVE THIS WIZARD UNTIL I KNOW **ALL** HIS **MAGICAL SECRETS**...

...THEN I'LL **DISPOSE** OF HIM!

ONE DAY, ARTHUR IS RIDING IN THE FOREST WHEN...

STOP, SIRE!

MERLIN?

I'VE COME TO SAY **FAREWELL**, ARTHUR. I'M LEAVING CAMELOT, **NEVER TO RETURN**.

WHAT? I **FORBID** IT!

MY **DESTINY** LIES WITH **LADY NIMUE**.

CAN SHE BE **TRUSTED**?

LOVE IS THE ONE THING THAT **BLINDS** MY POWERS. I **MUST** TRUST HER.

BUT **MERLIN**...

33

NO DISCUSSIONS. JUST HEAR MY **WARNING!** BEWARE OF THE **EVIL WOMAN** WHO WILL ONE DAY **STEAL** EXCALIBUR...

...AND HER **SON** WHO WILL **STRIKE YOU DOWN!**

THIS WOMAN WILL BE WITH YOU AT **THE END,** WHEN HER HEART IS **WASHED** OF ITS **EVIL.**

NOW I MUST BID YOU FAREWELL!

CAN SUCH TERRIBLE DAYS **TRULY** LIE AHEAD?

FAREWELL OLD FRIEND. I CAN ONLY HOPE THAT, JUST THIS ONCE, YOU'RE **WRONG.**

MERLIN JOINS NIMUE AND THEY TRAVEL ACROSS THE KINGDOM. AS EACH DAY PASSES, SHE LEARNS MORE OF HIS SECRETS. THEN ONE DAY...

YOU, THE **DARK-HAIRED** BOY! **COME HERE!**

37

WHILE LANCELOT STRUGGLES WITH HIS CONSCIENCE, SOME AT CAMELOT HAVE ACTUALLY TURNED AGAINST ARTHUR...

THE KING'S HALF-SISTER, MORGAN LE FAY, HAS MYSTICAL POWERS. NOW SHE PLANS TO USE THEM AGAINST HER BROTHER, WITH THE HELP OF SIR ACCOLON...

OUR MEETING MUST BE **QUICK**. ARTHUR **KNOWS** OF MY POWERS AND IS **SUSPICIOUS** ABOUT MY **AMBITIONS**. WE MAY BE DISCOVERED AT **ANY MOMENT**.

SOON I WILL ASK YOU TO **FIGHT** FOR ME, ACCOLON. WILL YOU DO THAT?

TO THE DEATH! I'D SLAY **ANYONE** FOR YOUR LOVE.

EVEN THE **KING HIMSELF?**

IF YOU **WISHED** IT...

THANK YOU, MY LOVE. NOW **GO**, AND AWAIT MY **COMMAND**.

WELCOME, BOLD KNIGHTS!

COME **DINE** ON THE **FINEST FOOD**...

...WHILE WE **SERENADE** YOU.

THE TWO MEN FIND THEMSELVES UNABLE TO RESIST.

AFTER DINNER, THEY ARE LED TO THEIR OWN CABINS...

...WHERE THEY DRIFT INTO A DEEP... **DEEP**... SLEEP...

SPLASH!

MORGAN RIDES ON, DESPERATELY, OUT OF THE FOREST...

...AND INTO A STONY VALLEY...

ONE YEAR LATER, ARTHUR AND HIS KNIGHTS ARE FEASTING AT THE ROUND TABLE. BUT AS USUAL, ONE CHAIR REMAINS EMPTY – THE SO-CALLED 'PERILOUS SEAT'...

...THIS SEAT IS RESERVED FOR THE FINEST KNIGHT IN THE WORLD. IT'S SAID THAT ANY OTHER KNIGHT WHO SITS THERE WILL DIE.

SUDDENLY, SUPERNATURAL LETTERS OF FIRE APPEAR ON THE CHAIR...

A knight destined for greatness shall come to this chair...

A knight destined for greatness shall come to this chair...

THE SEAT TRULY IS **ENCHANTED**!

MOMENTS LATER...

GREETINGS, YOUR MAJESTY. MY NAME IS **NACIENS**.

THIS IS MY WARD, **GALAHAD**. HE'S COME TO TAKE HIS PLACE AT THE ROUND TABLE.

IS HE A **KNIGHT**?

I TOO!

AND I!

AND ME!

SOON EVERY KNIGHT HAS PLEDGED TO FIND THE GRAIL.

ARTHUR'S HEART SWELLS WITH PRIDE AS HIS KNIGHTS SPREAD OUT ACROSS THE KINGDOM ON THEIR QUEST...

GOOD FORTUNE TO YOU ALL!

PERCIVAL RIDES EAST. DAYS PASS, THEN ONE MORNING, HE SEES A GROUP OF RIDERS APPROACHING...

PERHAPS THESE MEN CAN **HELP** ME WITH MY **QUEST...**

BUT AS THE RIDERS COME CLOSER, IT BECOMES CLEAR THEY ARE FAR FROM FRIENDLY...

63

FOR A WHILE, ARTHUR'S KINGDOM REMAINS AT PEACE.

BUT BEHIND THE SCENES, MANY IN COURT ARE JEALOUS OF THEIR FELLOW KNIGHTS...

ONE EVENING, SIR AGRAVAIN IS WALKING IN THE CASTLE GARDENS, WHEN...

LANCELOT! ALONE WITH THE QUEEN!

SO THE WHISPERS I'VE HEARD ABOUT THEIR ROMANCE ARE TRUE!

AT LAST, A CHANCE FOR ME TO GET RID OF THAT ARROGANT KNIGHT, LANCELOT.

AGRAVAIN TAKES THE NEWS TO MORGAN LE FAY'S SON, MORDRED ...

THE KING MUST BE TOLD AT ONCE!

THIS COULD BE THE FIRST STEP TO AVENGING MY MOTHER AND SEIZING THE THRONE!

SOON MORDRED IS THE ONLY SURVIVOR. BADLY WOUNDED, HE HAS NO CHOICE BUT TO FLEE...

THE KING WILL WANT US **BOTH** DEAD NOW. **RUN AWAY WITH ME!**

I CAN'T! GO, LANCELOT, BUT DON'T FORGET ME.

WHILE LANCELOT ESCAPES, MORDRED TELLS THE KING WHAT HAS HAPPENED...

THEN THE FELLOWSHIP OF THE ROUND TABLE IS **BROKEN!**

YET LANCELOT WAS A **POPULAR** MAN. MANY KNIGHTS ARE SURE TO SIDE WITH HIM.

AND WHAT OF THE **QUEEN?** TREASON IS PUNISHABLE BY **DEATH,** YOUR MAJESTY.

I KNOW THAT **ONLY TOO WELL.**

MEANWHILE, BACK IN ENGLAND, MORDRED IS GRADUALLY GAINING THE RESPECT OF THE YOUNG KNIGHTS. EVENTUALLY HE FEELS BOLD ENOUGH TO MAKE AN ANNOUNCEMENT...

I HAVE **GRAVE** NEWS FROM FRANCE. HIS MAJESTY KING ARTHUR HAS BEEN **KILLED!**

ARTHUR PASSED COMMAND TO **ME**. I NOW CLAIM MY RIGHT TO **RULE** AS HIS **HEIR!**

MORDRED IS QUICKLY CROWNED KING. AFTER THE CEREMONY, HE SEEKS OUT GUINEVERE...

I AM **KING** NOW, SO YOU MUST MARRY ME!

I JUST **KNOW** ARTHUR IS STILL ALIVE! I HAVE TO GET **WORD** TO HIM SOMEHOW.

WITH HER TRUSTED KNIGHTS BY HER SIDE, GUINEVERE FLEES ACROSS THE COUNTRY TO A FORTRESS IN LONDON, WHERE SHE TAKES REFUGE...

MORDRED SOON REALIZES HIS ARMY IS IN DANGER OF DEFEAT...

RETREAT!

HE SWIFTLY LEADS HIS MEN AWAY...

...BUT ARTHUR'S ARMY TRACKS THEM DOWN.

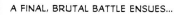
A FINAL, BRUTAL BATTLE ENSUES...

SOON ONE HUNDRED THOUSAND KNIGHTS LIE DEAD.

I MUST GO IN AND PRAY FOR GUINEVERE.

SIR BEDEVERE!

I NEEDN'T ASK WHOSE GRAVE YOU ATTEND.

LANCELOT JOINS BEDEVERE'S VIGIL AT ARTHUR'S RESTING PLACE...

SHORTLY AFTERWARDS, ARTHUR'S BELOVED GUINEVERE LEAVES THIS WORLD AND IS PLACED ALONGSIDE HER KING BY THE FAITHFUL LANCELOT.

SOON, BOTH HE AND BEDEVERE, THE LAST OF THE KNIGHTS OF THE ROUND TABLE, ARE NO MORE.

SOME SAY THAT ONE DAY, WHEN ARTHUR'S KINGDOM NEEDS HIM, HE WILL RETURN.

UNTIL THAT TIME, HE SLEEPS...

...IN A HIDDEN CORNER OF A FORGOTTEN FOREST...

...WHERE HIS TOMBSTONE TELLS OF A LEGENDARY RULER, WAITING TO LIVE ONCE MORE...

HERE LIES ARTHUR, THE ONCE AND FUTURE KING

THE END

The Legend of King Arthur

T ales of King Arthur and his knights have been told for hundreds of years. But are they merely stories, or was Arthur a real ruler of Ancient Britain?

Some of the earliest known mentions of Arthur come from Welsh and Breton stories and poems of the 5th and 6th centuries.

Arthur's role in these tales varies. In some, his enemies are Saxon invaders. In others they are dragons, giants and witches. Certain poems link Arthur with Annwn, the Welsh Otherworld, a place separate from everyday reality. Arthur is also mentioned in Welsh Triads, which were written descriptions of Welsh folklore, mythology and traditional history.

Probably the most significant account of Arthur's life and times came in *Historia Regum Britanniae* (*History of the Kings of Britain*). This was a semi-historical account of British history up to the 7th century, written around 1136 by Geoffrey of Monmouth.

Geoffrey's retelling portrays Arthur as the King of Britain who defeats Saxon invaders before building an empire. The tale mentions Uther Pendragon, Arthur's father, as well as many of the other figures associated with the legend, such as Merlin, Guinevere, Kay, Bedevere and Mordred, along with the sword Excalibur.

A French writer named Chrétien de Troyes wrote five Arthurian romances between 1170 and 1190. These introduced Lancelot and the Holy Grail to the story, together with a passing reference to Camelot, the castle at the heart of Arthur's kingdom.

The first half of the 13th century saw the Vulgate Cycle of stories: five French works which introduced the character of Galahad, developed Merlin's role and established Camelot as King Arthur's court.

In the late 15th century, English writer Thomas Malory retold the whole legend in *Le Morte d'Arthur*. Malory based his story on the previous romances, in particular the Vulgate Cycle. When it was published in 1485, *Le Morte d'Arthur* was one of the earliest printed books in England.

After the end of the Middle Ages, the Arthurian legend fell out of popularity. When it did make an appearance – as in *The History of Tom Thumb* – it tended to be treated less seriously. Published in 1621, *Tom Thumb* was the first fairy tale to be printed in English and it featured the tiny hero entertaining King Arthur's court.

In *The Lady of Shalott*, the heroine travels to Camelot, but dies before she can enter the castle.

The 19th century, however, brought a revival in interest in the legend. *Le Morte d'Arthur* was published in 1816 for the first time since 1634.

Alfred Lord Tennyson, Poet Laureate of Great Britain and Ireland, wrote several Arthurian poems including *The Lady of Shalott*, first published in 1832, and *Sir Lancelot and Queen Guinevere*, published ten years later. He went on to write *Idylls of the King*, published between 1859 and 1885, a series of twelve poems which covered Arthur's entire life.

Arthurian legend inspired other poets and writers, such as William Wordsworth (1770-1850) and William Morris (1834-1896), as well as artists such as Edward Burne-Jones who painted *The Last Sleep of Arthur in Avalon* between 1881 and 1898. In America, author Sidney Lanier wrote *The Boy's King Arthur* (1880) and the legend became the inspiration for Mark Twain's *A Connecticut Yankee in King Arthur's Court* (1889).

Later retellings included T.H. White's *The Once and Future King* (1958), which was loosely taken from *Le Morte d'Arthur* and was adapted into a stage musical, *Camelot* (1960), and a Disney animated feature film, *The Sword in the Stone* (1963).

Other film versions of the legend include *Camelot* (1967), *First Knight* (1995) and *King Arthur* (2004).

There have also been numerous television adaptations over the years, including *The Adventures of Sir Lancelot* (1956–57), *Arthur of the Britons* (1972–1973), *The Legend of King Arthur* (1979), *Merlin* (2008–2012) and *Camelot* (2011).

So did King Arthur really exist? Some people believe so. *The Historia Brittonum*, a history of Britain written around the year 828, lists twelve battles fought by Arthur. But it doesn't refer to him as a king and some historians have questioned its reliability.

Arthurian characters are also referred to in the *Annales Cambriae*, a chronicle of British history compiled from the 10th to 13th centuries, but many other contemporary histories make no mention of Arthur at all.

It's thought by some that Glastonbury in the county of Somerset is the site of the Isle of Avalon. Among the ruins of Glastonbury Abbey are tombstones which claim to mark the final resting place of Arthur and Guinevere.

However, most historians think it unlikely that the King Arthur of legend really existed, or argue at least that real evidence has yet to emerge.

Russell Punter was born in Bedfordshire, England. From an early age he enjoyed writing and illustrating his own stories. He trained as a graphic designer at art college in West Sussex before entering publishing in 1987. He has written over fifty books for children, ranging from original rhyming stories to adaptations of classic novels.

Andrea da Rold was born in Milan, Italy. He graduated from Milan's prestigious Academy of Fine Arts, and he still lives in the city today. He works as a cartoonist for Star Comics (*Samuel Sand, Lazarus Ledd*) and as an illustrator of children's books, working with, among others, Mondadori, De Agostini and Giunti. He illustrates the covers of the very popular *Geronimo Stilton* for Piemme and collaborates on Mondadori's *Focus Jr.* magazine.

Mike Collins has been creating comics for over 25 years. Starting on *Spider-Man* and *Transformers* for Marvel UK, he has also worked for DC, 2000AD and a host of other publishers. In that time he's written or drawn almost all the major characters for each company – *Wonder Woman, Batman, Superman, Flash, Teen Titans, X-Men, Captain Britain, Judge Dredd, Sláine, Rogue Trooper, Darkstars, Peter Cannon: Thunderbolt* and more. He currently draws a series of noir crime fiction graphic novels, *Varg Veum*. He also provides storyboards for TV and films, including *Doctor Who, Sherlock, Igam Ogam, Claude, Hana's Helpline* and *Horrid Henry*.

Cover design: Matt Preston

First published in 2017 by Usborne Publishing Ltd., Usborne House, 83-85 Saffron Hill, London EC1N 8RT, England. www.usborne.com
Copyright © 2017 Usborne Publishing Ltd.

All rights reserved. No part of this publication may be reproduced, stored in a retrieval system or transmitted in any form or by any means, electronic, mechanical, photocopying, recording or otherwise, without the prior permission of the publisher. The name Usborne and the devices ♀⊕ are Trade Marks of Usborne Publishing Ltd. UE. First published in America in 2017.